# The Dog Show

by Jill Atkins and Rupert Van Wyk

## W
## FRANKLIN WATTS
### LONDON•SYDNEY

On Monday, Dad met Isabel and Thomas from school.

"Look, Dad!" said Isabel.

"There is a Dog Show on Saturday."

"Can we take Scamp?" asked Thomas.

"Scamp is too naughty," said Dad.

"No he isn't," said the children.

"He just likes making people laugh."

"Well, you will have to train him," said Dad.

Isabel and Thomas began to train Scamp.

"Sit!" said Thomas, but Scamp lay down.

"Lie down," said Isabel,

but Scamp rolled over.

"Roll over," said Thomas,

but Scamp sat still.

"Sit still!" said Isabel,

but Scamp licked her hand.

Isabel and Thomas trained Scamp

all week long.

They trained him to fetch a toy,

and jump through a hoop.

By Friday, Scamp could do all the tricks.

"Good boy, Scamp!" laughed Isabel.

That night, she gave him a bath.

On Saturday, Isabel brushed Scamp's coat.

"He looks very smart," smiled Thomas.

They set off for the Dog Show.

"Do you think Scamp will win?" asked Isabel.

"I think so," said Thomas.

"We have trained him well."

The first class was for the smartest dog.

Isabel took Scamp into the ring.

"You look very smart, Scamp," called Thomas.

Scamp walked round the ring

with his head held high.

But then, he tripped and fell in the mud.

Everyone laughed.

Scamp liked making the people laugh.

He rolled over and over in the mud,

and everyone laughed again.

"Oh, Scamp!" cried Isabel.

"Never mind, Scamp. You did your best,"

said Thomas.

Next, the dogs had to do tricks.

The other dogs did everything right.

But Scamp wanted to make people laugh.

"Sit!" said Thomas, but Scamp lay down.

"Lie down," said Isabel,

but Scamp rolled over.

"Roll over," said Thomas,

but Scamp sat still.

"Sit still!" said Isabel,

but Scamp licked her hand.

Everyone laughed.

Next, it was the 'Fetch a toy' competition.

"Come on, Scamp. You are good at this,"
said Thomas.

Scamp ran round and round the ring,
looking for the toy. But he couldn't find it.

Thomas ran after him
and everyone laughed again.

"Never mind, Scamp," said Isabel.

"It is the obstacle race next.

You're good at that. I'm sure you will win."

Scamp liked making the people laugh.

They laughed when he ran around

the hoop, not inside it.

12

They laughed when he jumped
over the ladder.

But Isabel and Thomas looked sad.

They went to sit down
at the side of the park.
"Scamp didn't win any of the competitions,"
said Isabel.
"He forgot everything we did at home,"
said Thomas.

Scamp looked at Isabel and Thomas.

Why were they sad?

The people had laughed at him,

and it had been fun.

Isabel tickled Scamp's tummy.

"Never mind, you did your best,"

she said.

Thomas hugged Scamp.

"We still love you," he smiled.

Scamp licked his hand.

Suddenly, there was a loud voice.

"Scamp and his owners, please come back
to the ring."

Thomas and Isabel jumped up.

"Oh dear," said Isabel.

"Scamp must be in trouble

for getting everything wrong."

The judge came towards them.

"Scamp wins a special prize

for making everyone laugh," he said.

He fixed a red rosette to Scamp's collar.

Everyone clapped as Scamp trotted
round the ring, wagging his tail.
"Well done, Scamp," said Isabel.
"You did win, after all!"

# Story order

Look at these 5 pictures and captions.
Put the pictures in the right order
to retell the story.

**1**

Scamp is called back to the ring.

**2**

Isabel and Thomas are disappointed.

**3**

Scamp wins a rosette after all.

**4**

The family spot a poster.

**5**

Scamp likes making people laugh.

# Independent Reading

This series is designed to provide an opportunity for your child to read on their own. These notes are written for you to help your child choose a book and to read it independently.

In school, your child's teacher will often be using reading books which have been banded to support the process of learning to read. Use the book band colour your child is reading in school to help you make a good choice. *The Dog Show* is a good choice for children reading at Purple Band in their classroom to read independently.

The aim of independent reading is to read this book with ease, so that your child enjoys the story and relates it to their own experiences.

## About the book

Isabel and Thomas are excited about entering their dog, Scamp, in the local Dog Show. Despite all their training, Scamp doesn't get the tricks right. He just want to make people laugh. But can that also be worthy of a prize?

## Before reading

Help your child to learn how to make good choices by asking:
"Why did you choose this book? Why do you think you will enjoy it?"
Look at the cover together and ask: "What do you think the story will be about?" Ask your child to think of what they already know about the story context. Then ask your child to read the title aloud. Ask: "What sorts of things usually happen at a dog show?" Remind your child that they can sound out the letters to make a word if they get stuck.
Decide together whether your child will read the story independently or read it aloud to you.

## During reading

Remind your child of what they know and what they can do independently. If reading aloud, support your child if they hesitate or ask for help by telling the word. If reading to themselves, remind your child that they can come and ask for your help if stuck.

## After reading

Support comprehension by asking your child to tell you about the story. Use the story order puzzle to encourage your child to retell the story in the right sequence, in their own words. The correct sequence can be found on the next page.

Help your child think about the messages in the book that go beyond the story and ask: "Do you think Isabel and Thomas were right to be disapointed with Scamp? Why/Why not?"

Give your child a chance to respond to the story: "How do you think Isabel and Thomas felt before and after the dog show? Which part of the story was your favourite?"

## Extending learning

Help your child think more about the inferences in the story by asking: "Do you think the children would enter Scamp in another dog show? Explain why they would or would not do so."

In the classroom, your child's teacher may be teaching how to use speech marks to show when characters are speaking. There are many examples in this book that you could look at with your child. Find these together and point out how the end punctuation (comma, full stop, question mark or exclamation mark) comes inside the speech mark. Ask the child to read some examples out loud, adding appropriate expression.

Franklin Watts
First published in Great Britain in 2018
by The Watts Publishing Group

Copyright © The Watts Publishing Group 2018
All rights reserved.

Series Editors: Jackie Hamley and Melanie Palmer
Series Advisors: Dr Sue Bodman and Glen Franklin
Series Designer: Peter Scoulding

A CIP catalogue record for this book is
available from the British Library.

ISBN 978 1 4451 6230 0 (hbk)
ISBN 978 1 4451 6232 4 (pbk)
ISBN 978 1 4451 6231 7 (library ebook)

Printed in China

Franklin Watts
An imprint of
Hachette Children's Group
Part of The Watts Publishing Group
Carmelite House
50 Victoria Embankment
London EC4Y 0DZ

An Hachette UK Company
www.hachette.co.uk

www.franklinwatts.co.uk

**Answer to Story order: 4, 5, 2, 1,3**